The Young

E. W. Hornung

Alpha Editions

This edition published in 2024

ISBN : 9789362999863

Design and Setting By
Alpha Editions
www.alphaedis.com
Email - info@alphaedis.com

As per information held with us this book is in Public Domain. This book is a reproduction of an important historical work. Alpha Editions uses the best technology to reproduce historical work in the same manner it was first published to preserve its original nature. Any marks or number seen are left intentionally to preserve its true form.

Contents

CONSECRATION .... - 1 -
LORD'S LEAVE .... - 2 -
LAST POST .... - 4 -
THE OLD BOYS .... - 7 -
RUDDDY YOUNG GINGER .... - 9 -
THE BALLAD OF ENSIGN JOY .... - 12 -
BOND AND FREE .... - 37 -
SHELL-SHOCK IN ARRAS .... - 41 -
THE BIG THING .... - 42 -
FORERUNNERS * .... - 46 -
UPPINGHAM SONG .... - 48 -
WOODEN CROSSES .... - 51 -

CONSECRATION

    CHILDREN we deemed you all the days
We vexed you with our care:
But in a Universe ablaze,
What was your childish share?
To rush upon the flames of Hell,
To quench them with your blood!
To be of England's flower that fell
Ere yet it brake the bud!

And we who wither where we grew,
And never shed but tears,
As children now would follow you
Through the remaining years;
Tread' in the steps we thought to guide,
As firmly as you trod;
And keep the name you glorified
Clean before matt and God.

LORD'S LEAVE

(1915)

NO Lord's this year: no silken lawn on which
A dignified and dainty throng meanders.
The Schools take guard upon a fierier pitch
Somewhere in Flanders.

Bigger the cricket here; yet some who tried
In vain to earn a Colour while at Eton
Have found a place upon an England side
That can't be beaten!

A demon bowler's bowling with his head—
His heart's as black as skins in Carolina!
Either he breaks, or shoots almost as dead
As Anne Regina;

While the deep-field-gun, trained upon your stumps,
From concrete grand-stand far beyond the bound'ry,
Lifts up his ugly mouth and fairly pumps
Shells from Krupp's foundry.

But like the time the game is out of joint—
No screen, and too much mud for cricket lover;
Both legs go slip, and there's sufficient point
In extra cover!

Cricket? 'Tis Sanscrit to the super-Hun—
Cheap cross between Caligula and Cassius,
To whom speech, prayer, and warfare are all one—
Equally gaseous!

Playing a game's beyond him and his hordes;
Theirs but to play the snake or wolf or vulture:
Better one sporting lesson learnt at Lord's
Than all their Kultur....

Sinks a torpedoed Phoebus from our sight;
Over the field of play see darkness stealing;
Only in this one game, against the light
There's no appealing.

Now for their flares... and now at last the stars...
Only the stars now, in their heavenly million,
Glisten and blink for pity on our scars
From the Pavilion.

LAST POST

(1915)

LAST summer, centuries ago,
I watched the postman's lantern glow,
As night by night on leaden feet
He twinkled down our darkened street.

So welcome on his beaten track,
The bent man with the bulging sack!
But dread of every sleepless couch,
A whistling imp with leathern pouch!

And now I meet him in the way,
And earth is Heaven, night is Day,
For oh! there shines before his lamp
An envelope without a stamp!

Address in pencil; overhead,
The Censor's triangle in red.
Indoors and up the stair I bound:
One from the boy, still safe, still sound!

"Still merry in a dubious trench
They've taken over from the French;
Still making light of duty done;
Still full of Tommy, Fritz, and fun!

Still finding War of games the cream,
And his platoon a priceless team—

Still running it by sportsman's rule,
Just as he ran his house at school.

"Still wild about the 'bombing stunt'
He makes his hobby at the front.
Still trustful of his wondrous luck—
Prepared to take on old man Kluck!'"

Awed only in the peaceful spells,
And only scornful of their shells,
His beaming eye yet found delight
In ruins lit by flares at night,

In clover field and hedgerow green,
Apart from cover or a screen,
In Nature spurting spick-and-span
For all the devilries of Man.

He said those weeks of blood and tears
Were worth his score of radiant years.
He said he had not lived before—
Our boy who never dreamt of War!

He gave us of his own dear glow,
Last summer, centuries ago.
Bronzed leaves still cling to every bough.
I don't waylay the postman now.

Doubtless upon his nightly beat

He still comes twinkling down our street.

I am not there with straining eye—

A whistling imp could tell you why.

THE OLD BOYS

(1917)

WHO is the one with the empty sleeve?"
"Some sport who was in the swim."
"And the one with the ribbon who's home on leave?"
"Good Lord! I remember *him!*
A hulking fool, low down in the school,
And no good at games was he—
All fingers and thumbs—and very few chums.
(I wish he'd shake hands with me!)"

"Who is the one with the heavy stick,
Who seems to walk from the shoulder?"
"Why, many's the goal you have watched him kick!"
"He's looking a lifetime older.
Who is the one that's so full of fun—
I never beheld a blither—
Yet his eyes are fixt as the furrow betwixt?"
"He cannot see out of either,"

"Who are the ones that we cannot see,
Though we feel them as near as near?
In Chapel one felt them bend the knee,
At the match one felt them cheer.
In the deep still shade of the Colonnade,
In the ringing quad's full light,
They are laughing here, they are chaffing there,

Yet never in sound or sight."

"Oh, those are the ones who never shall leave,
As they once were afraid they would!
They marched away from the school at eve,
But at dawn came back for good,
With deathless blooms from uncoffin'd tombs
To lay at our Founder's shrine.
As many are they as ourselves to-day,
And their place is yours and mine."

"But who are the ones they can help or harm?"
"Each small boy, never so new,
Has an Elder Brother to take his arm,
And show him the thing to do—
And the thing to resist with a doubled fist,
If he'd be nor knave nor fool—
And the Game to play if he'd tread the way
Of the School behind the school."

RUDDDY YOUNG GINGER

(1915)

RUDDY young Ginger was somewhere in camp,
War broke it up in a day,
Packing cadets of the steadier stamp
Home with the smallest delay.

Ginger braves town in his O.T.C. rags—
Beards a Staff Marquis—the limb!
Saying, "Your son, Sir, is one of my fags,"
Gets a Commission through him.

Then to his tailor's for khaki *complet*;
Then to Pall Mall for a sword;
Lastly, a wire to his people to say,
"Left school—joined the Line—are you bored?"

And it *was* a bit cool
(A term's fees in the pool
By a rule of the school).
There were those who said "Fool!"
Of young Ginger.

Ruddy young Ginger! Who gave him that name?
Tommies who had his own nerve!
"Into 'im, Ginger!" was heard in a game
With a neighbouring Special Reserve.
Blushing and grinning and looking fifteen,

Ginger, with howitzer punt,
Bags his man's wind as succinctly and clean
As he hopes to bag Huns at the front.
Death on recruits who fall out by the way,
Sentries who yawn at their post,
Yet he sang such a song at the Y.M.C.A.
That the C.O. turned green as a ghost!

Less the song than the stance,
And the dissolute dance,
Drew a glance so askance
That... they packed him to France,
Little Ginger.

Next month, to the haunts of fine Ladies and
Lords
I ventured, in Grosvenor Square:
The stateliest chambers were hospital wards—
And ruddy young Ginger was there.
In spite of his hurts he looked never so red,
Nor ever less shy or sedate,
Though his hair had been cropped (by machine-
gun, he said)
And bandages turbaned his pate.

He was mostly in holes—but his cheek was
intact!
I could not but notice, with joy,
The loveliest Sisters had most to transact

With ruddy young Ginger—some boy!

Slaying Huns by the tons,
With a smile like a nun's—
Oh! of all the brave ones,
All the sons of our guns—
Give me Ginger!

THE BALLAD OF ENSIGN JOY

    I T is the story of
Ensign Joy
And the obsolete
rank withal
That I love for each gentle English
boy
Who jumped to his country's
call.
By their fire and fun, and the
deeds they've done,
I would gazette them Second to
none
Who faces a gun in Gaul!)

    IT is also the story of Ermyntrude
A less appropriate name
For the dearest prig and the
prettiest prude!
But under it, all the same,
The usual consanguineous squad
Had made her an honest child
of God—
And left her to play the game.

    IT was just when the grind of
the Special Reserves,
Employed upon Coast Defence,
Was getting on every Ensign's

nerves—
Sick-keen to be drafted
hence—
That they met and played tennis
and danced and sang,
The lad with the laugh and the
schoolboy slang,
The girl with the eyes intense.

    YET it wasn't for him that she
languished and sighed,
But for all of our dear deemed
youth;
And it wasn't for her, but her
sex, that he cried,
If he could but have probed
the truth !
Did she? She would none of his
hot young heart;
As khaki escort he's tall and
smart,
As lover a shade uncouth.

    HE went with his draft. She
returned to her craft.
He wrote in his merry vein:
She read him aloud, and the
Studio laughed!
Ermyntrude bore the strain.

He was full of gay bloodshed and
Old Man Fritz:
His flippancy sent her friends
into fits.
Ermyntrude frowned with
pain.

    HIS tales of the Sergeant who
swore so hard
Left Ermyntrude cold and
prim;
The tactless truth of the picture
jarred,
And some of his jokes were
grim.
Yet, let him but skate upon
tender ice,
And he had to write to her twice
or thrice
Before she would answer him.

    YET once she sent him a
fairy's box,
And her pocket felt the brunt
Of tinned contraptions and
books and socks—
Which he hailed as "a sporting
stunt!"
She slaved at his muffler none

the less,
And still took pleasure in mur-
muring, "Yes!
For a friend of mine at the
Front.")

    ONE fine morning his name
appears—
Looking so pretty in print!
"Wounded!" she warbles in
tragedy tears—
And pictures the reddening
lint,
The drawn damp face and the
draggled hair . . .
But she found him blooming in
Grosvenor Square,
With a punctured shin in a
splint.

    IT wasn't a haunt of Ermyn-
trude's,
That grandiose urban pile;
Like starlight in arctic altitudes
Was the stately Sister's smile.
It was just the reverse with
Ensign Joy—
In his golden greeting no least
alloy—

In his shining eyes no guile!

     HE showed her the bullet that
did the trick—
He showed her the trick,
x-ray'd;
He showed her a table timed to
a tick,
And a map that an airman
made.
He spoke of a shell that caused grievous loss—
But he never mentioned a certain
cross
For his part in the escapade!

     SHE saw it herself in a list next
day,
And it brought her back to his
bed,
With a number of beautiful
things to say,
Which were mostly over his
head.
Turned pink as his own pyjamas'
stripe,
To her mind he ceased to em-
body a type—
Sank into her heart instead.

I WONDER that all of you
didn't retire!"
"My blighters were not that
kind."
"But it says *you* 'advanced un-
der murderous fire,
Machine-gun and shell com-
bined—'"
"Oh, that's the regular War
Office wheeze!"
"'Advanced'—with that leg!—
'on his hands and knees'!"
"I couldn't leave it behind."

HE was soon trick-driving an
invalid chair,
and dancing about on a crutch;
The *haute noblesse* of Grosvenor
Square
Felt bound to oblige as such;
They sent him for many a motor-
whirl—
With the wistful, willowy wisp of
a girl
Who never again lost touch.

THEIR people were most of
them dead and gone.
They had only themselves to

His pay was enough to marry
upon,
As every Ensign sees.
They would muddle along (as
in fact they did)
With vast supplies of the *tertium*
quid
You bracket with bread-and-
cheese.
please.

    THEY gave him some leave
after Grosvenor Square—
And bang went a month on
banns;
For Ermyntrude had a natural
flair
For the least unusual plans.
Her heaviest uncle came down
well,
And entertained, at a fair hotel,
The dregs of the coupled clans.

    A CERTAIN number of
cheques accrued
To keep the wolf from the
door:
The economical Ermyntrude
Had charge of the dwindling

store,
When a Board reported her bridegroom fit
As—some expression she didn't permit . . .
And he left for the Front once more.

 HIS crowd had been climbing the jaws of hell:
He found them in death's dog-teeth,
With little to show but a good deal to tell
In their fissure of smoking heath.
There were changes—of course—but the change in him
Was the ribbon that showed on his tunic trim
And the tumult hidden beneath!

 FOR all he had suffered and seen before
Seemed nought to a husband's care;
And the Chinese puzzle of modern war

For subtlety couldn't compare
With the delicate springs of the complex life
To be led with a highly sensitised wife
In a slightly rarefied air!

    YET it's good to be back with the old platoon—
"A man in a world of men"!
Each cheery dog is a henchman boon—
Especially Sergeant Wren!
Ermyntrude couldn't endure his name—
Considered bad language no lien on fame,
Yet it's good to—hear it again!

    BETTER to feel the Sergeant's grip,
Though your fingers ache to the bone!
Better to take the Sergeant's tip
Than to make up your mind alone.
They can do things together, can Wren and Joy—

The bristly bear and the beard-
less boy—
That neither could do on his
own.

    BUT there's never a word
about Old Man Wren
In the screeds he scribbles
to-day—
Though he praises his N.C.O.'s
and men
In rather a pointed way.
And he rubs it in (with a knitted
brow)
That the war's as good as a pic-
nic now,
And better than any play!

    HIS booby-hutch is "as safe
as the Throne,"
And he fares "like the C.-in-
Chief,"
But has purchased "a top-hole
gramophone
By way of comic relief."
(And he sighs as he hears the
men applaud,
While the Woodbine spices are
wafted abroad

With the odour of bully-beef.)

     HE may touch on the latest type of bomb,
But Ermyntrude needn't blench,
For he never says where you hurl it from,
And it might be from your trench.
He never might lead a stealthy band,
Or toe the horrors of No Man's Land,
Or swim at the sickly stench. . . .

     HER letters came up by ration-cart
As the men stood-to before dawn:
He followed the chart of her soaring heart
With face transfigured yet drawn:
It filled him with pride, touched with chivalrous shame.
But—it spoilt the war, as a first-class game,
For this particular pawn.

THE Sergeant sees it, and damns the cause
In a truly terrible flow;
But turns and trounces, without a pause,
A junior N. C. O.
For the crime of agreeing that Ensign Joy
Isn't altogether the officer boy
That he was four months ago!

AT length he's dumfounded (the month being May)
By a sample of Ermyntrude's fun!
"You will kindly get leave *over* Christmas Day,
Or make haste and finish the
But Christmas means presents, she bids him beware:
"So what do you say to a son and heir?
I'm thinking of giving you Hun!"

WHAT, indeed, does the Ensign say?
What does he sit and write?

What do his heart-strings drone all day?
What do they throb all night?
What does he add to his piteous prayers?—
"Not for my own sake, Lord, but
—*theirs*,
See me safe through ..."

 THEY talk—and he writhes
—"of our spirit out here,
Our valour and all the rest!
There's my poor, lonely, delicate dear,
As brave as the very best!
We stand or fall in a cheery crowd,
And yet how often we grouse aloud!
She faces *that* with a jest!"

 HE has had no sleep for a day and a night;
He has written her half a ream;
He has Iain him down to wait for the light,
And at last come sleep—and a dream.
He's hopping on sticks up the

studio stair:
A telegraph-boy is waiting there,
And—that is his darling's
scream!

    HE picks her up in a tender
storm—
But how does it come to pass
That he cannot see his reflected
form
With hers in the studio glass?
"What's wrong with that mir-
ror?"' he cries.
But only the Sergeant's voice
replies:
"Wake up, Sir! The Gas—
the Gas!"

    IS it a part of the dream of
dread?
What are the men about?
Each one sticking a haunted
head
Into a spectral clout!
Funny, the dearth of gibe and
joke,
When each one looks like a pig
in a poke,
Not omitting the snout!

 THERE'S your mask, Sir! No time to lose!"
Ugh, what a gallows shape!
Partly white cap, and partly noose!
Somebody ties the tape.
Goggles of sorts, it seems, inset:
Cock them over the parapet,
Study the battlescape.

 ENSIGN JOY'S in the second line—
And more than a bit cut off;
A furlong or so down a green incline
The fire-trench curls in the trough.
Joy cannot see it—it's in the bed
Of a river of poison that brims instead.
He can only hear—a cough!

 NOTHING to do for the Companies there—
Nothing but waiting now,
While the Gas rolls up on the balmy air,
And a small bird cheeps on a

bough.
All of a sudden the sky seems full
Of trusses of lighted cotton-wool
And the enemy's big bow-
wow!

  THE firmament cracks with
his airy mines,
And an interlacing hail
Threshes the clover between our
lines,
As a vile invisible flail.
And the trench has become a
mighty vice
That holds us, in skins of molten
ice,
For the vapors that fringe the
veil.

  IT'S coming—in billowy swirls
—as smoke
From the roof a world on fire.
It—comes! And a lad with a
heart of oak
Knows only that heart's de-
sire!
His masked lips whimper but one
dear name—
And so is he lost to inward shame

That he thrills at the word:
"*Re-tire!*"

     WHOSE is the order, thrice renewed?
Ensign Joy cannot tell :
Only, that way lies Ermyntrude,
And the other way this hell!
Three men leap from the poisoned fosse,
Three men plunge from the parados,
And—their—officer—as well!

     NOW, as he flies at their flying heels,
He awakes to his deep disgrace,
But the yawning pit of his shame reveals
A way of saving his face:
He twirls his stick to a shepherd's crook,
To trip and bring one of them back to book,
As though he'd been giving chase!

     HE got back gasping—

"They'd too much start!"
"I'd've shot 'em instead!"
said Wren.
"That was your job, Sir, if you'd the 'eart—
But it wouldn't 've been you, then.
I pray my Lord I may live to see
A firing-party in front o' them three!"
(That's what he said to the men.)

NOW, Joy and Wren, of Company B,
Are a favourite firm of mine;
And the way they reinforced A, C, and D
Was, perhaps, not unduly fine;
But it meant a good deal both to Wren and Joy—
That grim, gaunt man, but that desperate boy!—
And it didn't weaken the Line.

NOT a bad effort of yours, my lad,"
The Major deigned to declare.
"My Sergeant's plan, Sir"—

"And that's not bad—
But you've lost that ribbon
you wear?"
"It—must have been eaten away
by the Gas!"
"Well—ribbons are ribbons—
but don't be an ass!
It's better to do than dare."

    DARE! He has dared to de-
sert his post—
But he daren't acknowledge
his sin!
He has dared to face Wren with
a lying boast—
But Wren is not taken in.
None sings his praises so long
and loud—
With look so loving and loyal
and proud!
But the boy sees under his
skin.

    DAILY and gaily he wrote to
his wife,
Who had dropped the beati-
fied droll
And was writing to him on the
Meaning of Life

And the Bonds between Body
and Soul.
Her courage was high—though
she mentioned its height;
She was putting upon her the
Armour of Light—
Including her aureole!

    BUT never a helm had the lad
we know,
As he went on his nightly raids
With a brace of his Blighters, an
N. G O.
And a bagful of hand-grenades
And the way he rattled and
harried the Hun—
The deeds he did dare, and the
risks he would run—
Were the gossip of the Bri-
gades.

    HOW he'd stand stockstill as
the trunk of a tree,
With his face tucked down
out of sight,
When a flare went up and the
other three
Fell prone in the frightening
light.

How the German sandbags, that made them quake,
Were the only cover he cared to take,
But he'd eavesdrop there all night.

    MACHINE-GUNS, tapping a phrase in Morse,
Grew hot on a random quest,
And swarms of bullets buzzed down the course
Like wasps from a trampled nest.
Yet, that last night!
They had just set off
When he pitched on his face with a smothered cough,
And a row of holes in his chest.

    HE left a letter. It saved the lives
Of the three who ran from the Gas;
A small enclosure alone survives,
In Middlesex, under glass:
Only the ribbon that left his breast
On the day he turned and ran

with the rest,
And lied with a lip of brass!

 BUT the letters they wrote
about the boy,
From the Brigadier to the
men!
They would never forget dear
Mr. Joy,
Not look on his like again.
Ermyntrude read them with dry,
proud eye.
There was only one letter that
made her cry.
It was from Sergeant Wren:

 THERE never was such a fear-
less man,
Or one so beloved as he.
He was always up to some daring
plan,
Or some treat for his men and
me.
There wasn't his match when he
went away;
But since he got back, there has
not been a day
But what he has earned a
V. C

A CYNICAL story? That's
not my view.
The years since he fell are
twain.
What were his chances of coming
through?
Which of his friends remain?
But Ermyntrude's training a
splendid boy
Twenty years younger than En-
sign Joy.
On balance, a British gain!

AND Ermyntrude, did she
lose her all
Or find it, two years ago?
O young girl-wives of the boys
who fall,
With your youth and your
babes to show!
No heart but bleeds for your
widowhood.
Yet Life is with you, and Life is
good.
No bone of *your* bone lies low!

YOUR blessedness came—as
it went—in a day.

Deep dread but heightened
your mirth.
Your idols' feet never turned to
clay—
Never lit upon common earth.
Love is the Game but is *not* the
Goal:
You played it together, body and
soul,
And you had your Candle's
worth.

    YES! though the Candle light
a Shrine,
And heart cannot count the
cost,
You are Winners yet in its tender
shine!
Would *they* choose to have
lived and lost?
There are chills, you see, for the
finest hearts;
But, once it is only old Death
that parts,
There can never come twinge
of frost.

    AND this be our comfort for
Every Boy

Cut down in his high heyday,
Or ever the Sweets of the Morning cloy,
Or the Green Leaf wither away;
So a sunlit billow curls to a crest,
And shouts as it breaks at its loveliest,
In a glory of rainbow spray!

 BE it also the making of Ermyntrude,
And many a hundred more—
Compact of foibles and fortitude—
Woo'd, won, and widow'd, in War.
God, keep us gallant and undefiled,
Worthy of Husband, Lover, or —Child...
Sweet as themselves at the core!

BOND AND FREE

(The Bapaume Road, *March* 1917)

MISTY and pale the sunlight, brittle and black the trees;
Roads powdered like sticks of candy for a car to crunch as they freeze...
Then we overtook a Battalion... and it wasn't a roadway then,
But cymbals and drums and dulcimers to the beat of the marching men!

They were laden and groomed for the trenches, they were shaven and scrubbed and fed;
Like the scales of a single Saurian their helmets rippled ahead;
Not a sorrowful face beneath them, just the tail of a scornful eye
For the car full of favoured mufti that went quacking and quaking by.

You gloat and take note in your motoring coat, and the sights come fast and thick:
A party of pampered prisoners, toying with shovel and pick;
A town where some of the houses are so many heaps of stone,
And some of them steel anatomies picked clean to the buckled bone.

A road like a pier in a hurricane of mountainous seas of mud,
Where a few trees, whittled to walking-sticks, rose out of the frozen flood
Like the masts of the sunken villages that might have been down below—
Or blown off the festering face of an earth that God Himself wouldn't know!

Not a yard but was part of a shell-hole—not an inch, to be more precise—
And most of the holes held water, and all the water was ice:
They stared at the bleak blue heavens like the glazed blue eyes of the slain,
Till the snow came, shutting them gently, and sheeting the slaughtered plain.

Here a pile of derelict rifles, there a couple of horses lay—
Like rockerless rocking-horses, as wooden of leg as they,
And not much redder of nostril—not anything like so grim
As the slinking ghoul of a lean live cat creeping over the crater's rim!

And behind and beyond and about us were the long black Dogs of War,

With pigmies pulling their tails for them, and making the monsters roar
As they slithered back on their haunches, as they put out their flaming tongues,
And spat a murderous message long leagues from their iron lungs!

They were kennelled in every corner, and some were in gay disguise,
But all kept twitching their muzzles and baying the silvery skies!
A howitzer like a hyena guffawed point-blank at the car—
But only the sixty - pounder leaves an absolute aural scar!

(Could a giant but crack a cable as a stockman cracks his whip,
Or tear up a mile of calico with one unthinkable r-r-r-r-rip!
Could he only squeak a slate-pencil about the size of this gun,
You might get some faint idea of its sound, which is those three sounds in one.)

But certain noises were absent, we looked for some sights in vain,
And I cannot tell you if shrapnel does really descend like rain—

Or Big Stuff burst like a bonfire, or bullets whistle or moan;
But the other figures I'll swear to—if some of 'em *are* my own!

Livid and moist the twilight, heavy with snow the trees,
And a road as of pleated velvet the colour of new cream-cheese...
Then we overtook a Battalion... and I'm hunting still for the word
For that gaunt, undaunted, haunted, whitening, frightening herd!

They had done their tour of the trenches, they were coated and caked with mud,
And some of them wore a bandage, and some of them wore their blood!
The gaps in their ranks were many, and none of them looked at me...
And I thought of no more vain phrases for the things I was there to see,
But I felt like a man in a prison van where the rest of the world goes Free.

SHELL-SHOCK IN ARRAS

ALL night they crooned high overhead
As the skies are over men:
I lay and smiled in my cellar bed,
And went to sleep again.

All day they whistled like a lash
That cracked in the trembling town:
I stood and listened for the crash
Of houses thundering down.

In, in they came, three nights and days,
All night and all day long;
It made us learned in their ways
And experts on their song.

Like a noisy clock, or a steamer's screw,
Their beat debauched the ear,
And left it dead to a deafening few
That burst who cared how near?
We only laughed when the flimsy floor
Heaved on the shuddering sod:
But when some idiot slammed a door—
My God!

THE BIG THING

(1918)

IT WAS a British Linesman. His face was like a fist,
His sleeve all stripes and chevrons from the elbow to the wrist.
Said he to an American (with other words of his):
"It's a big thing you are doing—do you know how big it is?"

"I guess, Sir," that American inevitably drawled,
"Big Bill's our proposition an' we're goin' for him bald.
You guys may have him rattled, but I figure it's for us
To slaughter, quarter, grill or bile, an' masticate the cuss."

"I hope your teeth," the Linesman said, "are equal to your tongue—
But that's the sort of carrion that's better when it's hung.
Yet—the big thing you're doing I should like to make you see!"
"Our stunt," said that young Yankee, "is to set the whole world free!"

The Linesman used a venial verb (and other parts of speech):

"That's just the way the papers talk and politicians preach!
But apart from gastronomical designs upon the Hun—
And the rather taller order—there's a big thing that you've *done*."

"Why, say! The biggest thing on earth, to any cute onlooker,
Is Old Man Bull and Uncle Sam aboard the same blamed hooker!
One crew, one port, one speed ahead, steel-true twin-hearts within her:
One ding-dong English-singin' race—a race without a winner!"

The boy's a boyish mixture—half high-brow and half droll:
So brave and naïve and cock-a-hoop—so sure yet pure of soul!
Behold him bright and beaming as the bride-groom after church—
The Linesman looking wistful as a rival in the lurch!

"I'd love to be as young as you—" he doesn't even swear—
"Love to be joining up anew and spoiling for my share!

But when your blood runs cold and old, and brain and bowels squirm,
The only thing to ease you is some fresh blood in the firm.

"When the war was young, and *we* were young, we felt the same as you:
A few short months of glory—and we didn't care how few!
French, British and Dominions, it took us all the same—
Who knows but what the Hun himself enjoyed his dirty game!

"We tumbled out of tradesmen's carts, we fell off office stools;
Fathers forsook their families, boys ran away from schools;
Mothers untied their apron-strings, lovers unloosed their arms—
All Europe was a wedding and the bells were war's alarms!

"The chime had changed—You took a pull—the old wild peal rings on
With the clamour and the glamour of a Generation gone.
Their fun—their fire—their hearts' desire—are born again in You!"

"*That* the big thing we're doin'?"

"It's as big as Man can do!"

FORERUNNERS *

(1900)

WHEN I lie dying in my bed,
A grief to wife, and child, and friend,—
How I shall grudge you gallant dead
Your sudden, swift, heroic end!

Dear hands will minister to me,
Dear eyes deplore each shallower breath:
You had your battle-cries, you three,
To cheer and charm you to your death.

You did not wane from worse to worst,
Under coarse drug or futile knife,
But in one grand mad moment burst
From glorious life to glorious Life....

These twenty years ago and more,
'Mid purple heather and brown crag,
Our whole school numbered scarce a score,
And three have fallen for the Flag.

   * *H. P. P.—F. M. J. W. A. C. St. Ninian's, Moffat, 1879-1880; South Africa, 1899-1900.*

You two have finished on one side,
You who were friend and foe at play;
Together you have done and died;
But that was where you learnt the way.

And the third face! I see it now,
So delicate and pale and brave.
The clear grey eye, the unruffled brow,
Were ripening for a soldier's grave.

Ah! gallant three, too young to die!
The pity of it all endures.
Yet, in my own poor passing, I
Shall lie and long for such as yours.

UPPINGHAM SONG

(1913)

AGES ago (as to-day they are reckoned)
I was a lone little, blown little fag:
Panting to heel when Authority beckoned,
Spoiling to write for the *Uppingham Mag.!*
Thirty years on seemed a terrible time then—
Thirty years back seems a twelvemonth or so.
Little I saw myself spinning this rhyme then—
Less do I feel that it's ages ago!

Ages ago that was Somebody's study;
Somebody Else had the study next door.
O their long walks in the fields dry or muddy!
O their long talks in the evenings of yore!
Still, when they meet, the old evergreen fellows
Jaw in the jolly old jargon as though
Both were as slender and sound in the bellows
As they were ages and ages ago!

O but the ghosts at each turn I could show you!—
Ghosts in low collars and little cloth caps—
Each of 'em now quite an elderly O.U.—
Wiser, no doubt, and as pleasant—perhaps!
That's where poor Jack lit the slide up with tollies,
Once when the quad was a foot deep in snow—
When a live Bishop was one of the Pollies * —

Ages and ages and ages ago!

Things that were Decent and things that were Rotten,
How I remember them year after year!
Some—it may be—that were better forgotten:
Some that—it may be—should still draw a tear...
More, many more, that are good to remember:
Yarns that grow richer, the older they grow:
Deeds that would make a man's ultimate ember
Glow with the fervour of ages ago!

Did we play footer in funny long flannels?
Had we no Corps to give zest to our drill?
Never a Gym lined throughout with pine panels?
Half of your best buildings were quarry-stone still?

   * *Præpostors.*
Ah! but it's not for their looks that you love them,
Not for the craft of the builder below,
But for the spirit behind and above them—
But for the Spirit of Ages Ago!

Eton may rest on her Field and her River.
Harrow has songs that she knows how to sing.
Winchester slang makes the sensitive shiver.

Rugby had Arnold, but never had Thring!

Repton can put up as good an Eleven.

Marlborough men are the fear of the foe.

All that I wish to remark is—thank Heaven

I was at Uppingham ages ago!

WOODEN CROSSES

(1917)

GO LIVE the wide world over—but when you come to die, .
A quiet English churchyard is the only place to lie!
I held it half a lifetime, until through war's mischance
I saw the wooden crosses that fret the fields of France.

A thrush sings in an oak-tree, and from the old square tower
A chime as sweet and mellow salutes the idle hour:
Stone crosses take no notice—but the little wooden ones
Are thrilling every minute to the music of the guns!

Upstanding at attention they face the cannonade,
In apple-pie alinement like Guardsmen on parade:
But Tombstones are Civilians who loll or sprawl or sway
At every crazy angle and stage of slow decay.

For them the Broken Column—in its plot of unkempt grass;
The tawdry tinsel garland safeguarded under glass;
And the Squire's emblazoned virtues, that would

overweight a Saint,
On the vault empaled in iron—scaling red for want of paint!

The men who die for England don't need it rubbing in;
An automatic stamper and a narrow strip of tin
Record their date and regiment, their number and their name—
And the Squire who dies for England is treated just the same.

So stand the still battalions: alert, austere, serene;
Each with his just allowance of brown earth shot with green;
None better than his neighbour in pomp or circumstance—
All beads upon the rosary that turned the fate of France!

Who says their war is over? While others carry on,
The little wooden crosses spell but the dead and gone?
Not while they deck a sky-line, not while they crown a view,
Or a living soldier sees them and sets his teeth anew!
The tenants of the churchyard where the singing

thrushes build
Were not, perhaps, all paragons of promise well fulfilled:
Some failed—through Love, or Liquor—while the parish looked askance.
But—you cannot *die* a Failure if you win a Cross in France!

The brightest gems of Valour in the Army's diadem
Are the V.C. and the D.S.O., M.C. and D.C.M.
But those who live to wear them will tell you they are dross
Beside the Final Honour of a simple Wooden Cross.